eXplicitTales:

Group Fun

The Collection

— ◆ —

Lolita Minx

eXplicitTales

CONTENTS

TAKING THE TEAM

Throughout the game, I had kept cheering Gary and his team mates on, knowing that with every passing goal, I got one step closer to a very special, rashly made promise. I had to admit, the few beers I'd had last night definitely played a part, but at the same time I knew the offer to service the entire team was something that had been on my mind for a while now. It felt bad, filthy, unspeakably slutty, and yet…

As the countdown began, only a miracle could prevent them from winning the game, as well as an afternoon with me. When those eleven men ran back from the field, their sweat glistening in the bright sunlight, I felt a shiver travel down my spine. Was I ready for this? I had to be.

"Hello, Love," Gary was slightly out of breath by the time he arrived at my seat, his ten mates in tow. "Ready?" He gave me a wink and again, I felt my stomach clench with nervous anticipation.

"I've never broken a promise yet." I said, while eyeing the others; Tom, with the messy mop of dirty blonde hair that no comb could ever tame, Ian, whose broad, muscular shoulders clearly betrayed his day job as a builder, Lee, who was the tamest of them all, but I was certain his calm, brown eyes hid a certain passion that would soon be unleashed on me.

I got up and followed them into the locker rooms. The men took off their shirts soon after entering, wiped their faces with them, before discarding them on the wooden benches lining the changing room. And then, one by one, they turned to face me, eager for their reward to be presented to them.

Gary and I had always had an unconventional relationship. We'd go out to the local pub, and after just two rounds we'd be unable to keep our hands off each other. I lost count of the number of times I'd pleasured him with my mouth in the toilets. Neither of us cared whether we were alone in there, of it someone ended up watching.

This time, Gary's team mates would do more than just watch. And rather than jealousy, I could see his lips curled up at the corners in pride. Everyone would get a taste of me - his woman - but I'd go home with him in the end. That was our arrangement.

I started unbuttoning my white shirt, revealing my ample cleavage which threatened to spill out of the bright red bra I'd worn for this occasion.

It didn't take long for everyone's eyes to be glued on

me. Nobody dared to make the first move, until Gary stepped forward and tugged hard on my shirt, ripping it off me. I wrapped my arms around myself instinctively, but it was more to tease than to actually cover up.

Gary circled around me, gave me a tight swat on my leather-clad ass.

"Ow!" I squealed, turning to look him in the eye.

"Lolita, it's time."

That dark stare I knew so intimately burned into my soul, setting my insides alight and made me gush sweet nectar into my panties.

I wiggled my ass to get out of the tight leather skirt, and there I was, standing in the middle of a locker room full of sweaty men, in just my bra and panties. And heels of course, can't ignore the heels.

Gary stepped up again, wrapping his hand firmly around the back of my neck and giving me a firm kiss on my lips, before nibbling on my bottom lip.

I moaned into his mouth, unable to hide my excitement about what was about to unfold.

He released me abruptly, and waved over to his two best friends, Tom and Lee, who neared me with an almost predator-like determination. My breaths grew shallow, and my heart started to pound.

"She is hot, your girl," Tom remarked, as he slipped his

hand into his shorts and started pumping his already semi-hard cock with his fist.

Lee next to him just nodded, and couldn't keep his eyes off my rack.

I was just starting to imagine them both, butt naked, running their hands off me, when a pair of hands behind me, grabbed me roughly and forced me onto my back on what felt like one of those benches. As soon as I gave in, I could see Gary's lustful grin hovering above my face.

"Time to lose those," he gestured down at my crotch, and almost straight away, Tom stepped forward and pulled my panties down with one swift tug. Gary meanwhile lifted me slightly, ridding me of my bra with equal speed.

The rest of the team huddled around us, as he held me down, and I felt something warm and slightly sticky being run over my thigh. Mike had his cock out, his face betraying his readiness as he continued to rub his veiny head over me, stopping every so often to get a few feverish pumps in.

Half a dozen hands spread my legs, and more of the team started to jerk off at the uninterrupted view of my shaven and already dripping pussy.

I didn't have time to consider if this was really what I wanted, everyone had made that choice for me.

All around me, the same familiar noise: skin rubbing on

slick cock. Some started slow, others couldn't wait to speed up. I didn't know where to look, when all of a sudden one particularly large cock ended up right in front of my face, pressing at my lips. I looked up to find Steve, Gary's especially large and well-endowed black mate grinning at me.

"Open up those pretty lips of yours, and show us a good time."

I could feel my eyes widen, because the thought of his cock filling my mouth took my excitement to a whole new level. I licked my lips in preparation, then gave the head of his big, black cock a generous slurp too.

It had been a while since I'd tasted a man other than Gary, and the more excited everyone around me got, the more I felt like this reward was more for me than for any of them.

I took Steve's solid shaft between my lips and started to suck, as he lent down and held me from the back of my head.

Meanwhile between my thighs someone - I couldn't be sure who - had started rubbing his hot, throbbing cock all over my swollen, slick clit. I moaned into Steve's cock, and sucked harder, causing him to groan.

After only moments of teasing, my pussy was swiftly filled by the big mystery cock, at which point I could barely stop myself from biting down. Tears filled my eyes as my tight channel stretched to accommodate the big cock that started to pound me.

A pair of hands ran over my bare tits, tweaking my nipples until I writhed in pleasure as well as sweet pain. I tried to relax as best I could when Steve pushed forward, forcing his cock beyond the bump in my throat, making it almost impossible not to gag.

I felt so filthy and disgusting, having all these football players violate me like this, and yet I couldn't get enough of it. This is what I had hoped for, when I dangled this carrot in front of them the night before the match. I knew they'd work their asses off on the field to make this happen, certainly the other team wouldn't have had this much motivation to win.

From the corner of my eye, I saw Gary standing off to the side, his hand firmly tugging on his already full sized erection. He gave me another one of those looks, the ones that mean I'm his no matter what. No matter who is plugging my holes at this moment.

Another pair of sticky hands grabbed hold of me, lifting me up from my hips. I instinctively placed my feet beside my ass on the bench, raising it slightly, but that was not enough for this particular football player.

"Let's get her up," his voice was raw with lust, as

further hands raised me upwards, forcing Steve's cock out of my mouth, then put me back down on top of someone.

This third cock firmly pressed up against back entrance. I was about to protest that it seemed way too thick to fit in there, when another schlong was hurriedly stuffed into my mouth. I tried to keep up, kicking and sucking Gary's dick when I felt my asshole give in to the persistent pressure on it and I was finally filled to the core in all holes.

I bounced up and down as the cock in my ass seemed to grow with every push, all the while another guy was balls deep in my pussy.

Someone grabbed my hand and placed it on their sack, while my other hand tried it's best to steady the cock that was roughly being shoved into the back of my throat. I was out of breath with exertion as well as pleasure when the first guy blew his load right in the centre of my chest. The sight of his slutty girl being jizzed on by another guy must have been too much for Gary, because he also exploded.

Hot cum gushed into the back of my throat. I did my best to swallow it all, but as the still pulsating cock slipped out from in between my lips, some of it ended up dribbling down my chin.

"God, you're fucking beautiful like that," someone off to my left remarked, as he furiously tugged at his dick, before rubbing it into the gooey mess between my tits. Even if I wanted to, all these hard, glistening bodies were surrounding me, overwhelming me so completely, that there was no way of knowing whose cock was whose.

The stud pounding me hard in my pussy was getting close, I could tell by the erratic twitch in his rhythm, which was quickly edging me closer to the brink as well. With hardly any warning, my cunt erupted into spasms coursing all through my body. I screamed out, muffled by hot man flesh, forcing its way deeper down my throat, as tears streamed down my cheek, mixed in with sweat - both mine, and that dripping off the steaming bodies surrounding me.

As if unwilling to let go, my insides clenched hard around the rod impaling me, milking it a few times in quick succession and forcing it into sweet release along with me.

"Holy fucking shit!" I tried to shout, to no avail, instead letting my hands squeeze down hard on whatever dick within reach.

While my orgasm continued to make me lose all motor control, a few more guys finished around me, covering more of my bare skin with their sticky cum. I was slick, slippery, coated properly. It was so filthy, so degrading, and I loved every second of it.

It was only when the guy I was on top of, started to move faster again, that I realised I was still filled to the brim from behind, and he was getting impatient. Bucking and thrusting underneath me, he fought hard to reach his climax, during which I noticed Gary, caressing and playing with himself to my side, ready for round two.

I could hardly catch my breath as he all but wrestled his way through the mass of naked bodies, arriving between my thighs shortly after and sticking his cock deeply into my creamy folds. Once again I felt like I was almost being spliced open, impaled on two fat dicks from both ends, while exhaustedly lapping up the last droplets of cum from a third. With a shudder, the player underneath me ground to a spectacular finale, digging his fingers deeply into the soft flesh of my hips. I cried out with him, as he creamed my backdoor, growing rigid one final time before flopping back down underneath me.

Gary took my hands, allowing me to lift myself, so that I was now suspended in the air with my legs wrapped tightly around his waist as he continued to fuck my brains out like never before.

"That's my girl," he whispered into my ear just before biting into my neck just the way I like it when we're playing rough.

"Let's show these guys why you're with me, huh?"

I felt a smile creep over my face, despite the exhaustion that had already set in, and he carried me off towards the wall of lockers. Harder and bigger than the first time around, Gary pounded into me at an immense speed, causing my ass to smack repeatedly against the metal locker doors.

I embraced him, transferring the mixture of assorted cum from my body onto his. He didn't seem to mind, wrapping his arms around me even tighter while continuing to thrust into me, impaling me on his thick, huge cock again and again, as his teammates watched us. Mesmerised they were, their eyes glazed over in lust, while their hands inevitably came back down to the same place, no matter how spent they were.

We were surrounded by a mass of pulsating flesh, their sole focus to make the most of this filthy spectacle in front of them. After all, there was no telling if they'd ever get this opportunity again, the chance to watch Gary and me entranced by one another, swept up in lust.

Once again, I felt my lower abdomen tighten with the promise of pleasure. My muscles were almost too weak to take me there, but with Gary's unrelenting strength, the scream of my final release filled the space around us. He joined me as I died another little death, my being arriving one step closer to nirvana. I was content. I was proud.

Gary's face tightened, his lips tightening to a thin line as he shuddered his last load into me, branding me his, no matter what had just occurred.

I slumped into his arms, it was beyond my ability to hang on to him as the muscles in my shoulders as well as my legs finally gave up. He scooped me up, nuzzling my sweaty locks and carried me towards the shower.

The locker room was filled with the smell of sweaty sex, the floor cum stained, as the other boys started picking up their things, and made a half-hearted attempt to eliminate the evidence of what had just happened.

"You did great, my goddess," Gary whispered in my ear, making me smile. "Let's get you cleaned up."

I could do no more but try to hang on to consciousness, as he held me underneath the warm shower, washing the strain and dirt away.

But nobody could wash away the memory of this day. The day I took on the whole team.

USED AT THE PUB

It had barely been a week since the orgy in Gary's team's locker room and the memories of that afternoon were still extremely vivid in my mind. Every so often I would catch myself recalling glimpses of the debauchery I was subjected to at the hands - or cocks - of Gary's mates and my heart would start hammering all over again. What was even better, Gary had been insatiable ever since, his usual passionate kiss to greet me when he got home from work had become more urgent, resulting in me being bent over the kitchen table more than once in the past week.

Tonight we were hell bent on celebrating again, nothing to do with sports, just a regular date night for the two of us. We were going to go for a quiet couple of drinks to our local pub, and then see where the night took us.

It turned out, we need not have looked further than the old pub for some good old fashioned fun. Neither did the other patrons.

Gary and I have always known how to have a good time and that night was no different. We had a few drinks, watched as some of the other regulars tried to settle an old score over the dartboard, and then he gave me that look.

That look, which I knew so well…

"What do you say, love, we take things somewhere more private," Gary whispered in my ear, after brushing a few locks out of my face.

I was glowing with anticipation - or the after effects of the Vodka-Redbull I'd been enjoying that evening. Either way, I was well up for it.

"Sure thing. So long as by more private, you mean not very private at all…" I winked at him and he broke his dark, brooding stare for only a moment, when a knowing grin appeared on his lips.

"You know me. That's always what I mean." Gary got up, and firmly took my hand, ready to lead me into the back of the pub. The bar was mostly quiet, with only a few people around who were engaged in deep conversation with one another. The ladies room would be free, I knew that already. The ladies room in this place was always free for us.

Gary fidgeted with his phone before putting it back in his pocket.

"What's going on?" I asked, but he just shook his head instead of responding.

Work perhaps, I thought. I was wrong, but I didn't' know it yet.

As soon as he led me inside, and I heard the door shut

behind it, his hands were on me. All over me. I closed my eyes as he started to suck on my neck, the delicious tickle was getting my juices running. Not that I'd been dry at all since the night at the football ground. No, my clit was a throbbing and constant reminder of all the pleasure I'd been subjected to. I couldn't get the memories out of my mind for more than minutes at a time, before they'd be back, pushing me to do it all over again.

I slipped my hand into Gary's trouser, pleased to find that he was equally ready. Of course Gary generally was. I don't think I've ever found him limp. The man could jackhammer me against a wall even if he was running a fever or otherwise in less than perfect condition.

He groaned in to my ear when I closed my fingers tightly around his thick girth and began to stroke him. Then, the biting started. He threaded his fingers through my hair and tugged my head further to the side. I loved having my hair pulled and he knew it.

Gary sucked on my neck, giving me just enough tooth action to make my skin raw. I loved every bit of the attention, even if I knew I'd have a bruise there in the morning. I didn't care.

His phone went off again, but before I could question him, he flipped me around and pressed me up against the plywood wall of the toilet stall, grinding his solid cock into my arse.

"Get ready, Lolita, you're gonna have a hell of a night." His breath against the side of my neck gave me goose bumps. Or perhaps those were caused by his hand, slipping underneath my skirt and cupping my cunt from behind.

I didn't get the chance to ask what was in store for me other than the usual fuck'n'suck in the pub bathroom, when I heard the door creak. That wasn't unusual. All the regulars knew that when we came in here together, there'd be quite the show for everyone. We didn't mind an audience, in fact it made us want to perform even harder.

But this time, it wasn't a quiet observer who came in, it was a familiar voice.

"Hey girl," Steve - Gary's mate from football, and my First Black Cock in a long time - said.

I visibly shivered hearing his voice. Steve was a total stud, and it started to dawn on me that he was likely here to participate again. I couldn't fucking wait.

"Hey Steve," I responded, gasping loudly when Gary let his finger slip past my thong and into my slick pussy.

"The others are on the way," Steve said in a tone that suggested he was talking to Gary. So that's what all the phone stuff had been about. Unbeknownst to me, Gary had set up a do-over on last week's gangbang.

I closed my eyes, trying to regain focus, but I was a quivering mess while Gary continued to finger-bang me. Every time I tried to move or look at what was going on behind me, he pushed me against the partition wall again, rendering me completely helpless.

My knees felt weak and my throat became dry. The anticipation of what was inevitably going to happen again was killing me.

The door creaked again, and a few more voices greeted us. My consciousness seemed to enter another level of existence. Things like saying hello, putting names with faces, didn't matter anymore. My mind became foggy and I was overcome with a crazy lust for cock.

Gary held me firmly in place still, while he peeled my tight skirt over my ass, exposing my ass to the spectators. I had worn my favourite black lace thong for the occasion and from the sounds of cocks getting slicked up, my audience appreciated the effort.

"Let me have a go first," Steve's deep voice broke through the background noise.

I closed my eyes, wishing that that would indeed happen. I loved Gary, he made me incredibly horny, but the feel of Steve's big black cock was something else altogether. I wanted to feel it again, to remind myself.

Gary's hold on me loosened, as he shuffled aside and

took his finger away, leaving my cunt painfully empty. I took a deep breath, preparing myself, when an already rock solid cock entered me roughly, filling my pussy to the brim.

Steve's big dick felt even huger from this angle than it had done last time, making me cry out when he rammed it in hard.

His large hands firmly gripped my hips as he gave me a few good thrusts against the wall, before dragging me a few steps backwards, allowing me to bend over and rest my arms against the wood. My cunt burned again from being stretched to its limits and I savoured the feeling. Soon I'd be so wet, I'd feel it a lot less.

I looked back, watching Steve plough into me, when out of nowhere, a naked cock was thrust against my lips, forcing me to part and take it into my mouth. Gary.

His eyes were feverish as he gazed down at me, sweat starting to collect on his brow.

"She has a beautiful ass, this one," another voice said behind us.

I involuntarily twitched when a finger made its way down my crack, pushing against my anus until it opened up, allowing it inside.

My breath was ragged, my heart still racing, as the mystery finger started to finger my ass. Gary grabbed me by the hair and forced me to change direction slightly, followed by Steve who was still fucking me from behind. Before I knew it, I was gagging on Gary's thick cock while he face fucked me, his rhythm perfectly in sync with Steve's at the back. I felt pressure build inside me, originating from my pussy as well as my ass, signalling that my first release was only moments away.

But my pleasure was roughly interrupted when Steve shuddered to a halt, slamming into me hard as his nuts forced a big load inside my cunt. I felt myself getting completely filled, as the cum threatened to gush back out when he pulled back. But it was not to be, because someone else was at the ready, forcing his cock inside of me as soon as Steve released my hips.

I looked up at Gary, who had sped up, pumping his big cock with my lips much faster than before. I could barely keep up with him, but thankfully he had continued to keep a tight grip on my head, preventing his rod from slipping out.

Whether because of the drinks earlier, or the filthy fantasy being played out all around me, I felt fucking high. I was reaching the nirvana of my own religion and the relentless pressure inside my stomach was back, building ever stronger until an orgasm would be inevitable.

The stranger behind me wasn't quite as well-endowed

as Steve had been, but he was still pretty thick and better yet, he was fresh and energetic. I didn't know if he was another football player, the groans that started to get louder and wilder behind me didn't sound familiar. For all I knew, he could be just a random guy who overheard us fucking in the ladies room and decided to join in.

This thought made me even hornier, as did Gary, who was at the end of his tether now, guzzling cum down my throat which I did my best to lick up and swallow. I opened my eyes to find his orgasm face, eyebrows pulled together in ecstasy, which sent me straight for the abyss myself.

The random cock behind me kept going, thrusting into me again and again, making my skin sting with every ball slap as my cunt spasmed and contracted, attempting to milk it of its essence, but above all, not let the mystery cock escape as I came hard.

My knees buckled, but I was held up by a pair of strong hands behind me, while Gary looked on with an expression of exhausted pride on his face. I was his. I would only be his, but tonight, I was everyone else's too.

It occurred to me how lucky I was to have a guy like him, who would let me be me, as slutty and free as I wanted to be. We lived for pleasure, Gary and I. Not responsibility, not money, just pleasure.

"I'd like to fuck her sweet ass again," now Tom, another one of Gary's football mates said behind us.

The finger that had been plundering my anus was swiftly removed, as was the cock that I had cum so hard on before. While mystery man stepped aside, I saw that indeed he was a complete stranger. I'd never seen the guy before that moment, when he presented me with his cum-covered cock.

I opened my mouth, ready to clean the mixture of juices off it with my tongue, when Tom stuck his rod inside my ass as promised, causing me to squeal. The intensity of his length filling me caused me to close my eyes and take a deep breath, but then I was ready to continue.

The tattooed stranger guided me towards his dick with his hand on my chin. I complied, and opened wide, tasting the mixture of salty sweetness coating his cock.

He groaned when I sucked him hard, letting my tongue explore the ridges and veins on the way out.

Tom behind us dug his fingers into my hips as he found his groove, and fucked my tight asshole until it adjusted to his impressive size, allowing him to slide in and out more quickly than before. Meanwhile, someone - not sure who - opened the back zip of my top until my bare back was exposed, running his hands over my skin, setting it on fire. The noises in the background suggested that I wasn't the only thing he was rubbing, he was jerking himself off simultaneously as well. His hands explored the contours of my back, before forcing the top aside and cupping my tits.

I still felt feverish when I felt a familiar twitch in my ass, signalling Tom's spectacular release. He pulled out, and a hot gush of cum landed right on my ass cheek, dribbling down my thigh. A groan next to me suggested that sight was too much for the guy spanking the monkey while feeling me up, and his hot load ended up on my side, running down my ribs.

It was filthy, degrading, and liberating all at once. My insides began to quiver again, but with both my holes being empty, I couldn't get there on my own.

Thankfully someone else stepped up behind me and rammed his throbbing cock into my cunt hard. It was already dribbling, but he still gave me a good few thrusts, sending me into my second orgasm of the evening.

This time, I was pretty much overcome. I wasn't able to stay upright, sinking onto my knees on the cold floor, surrounded by spent cocks, with just the one - tattooed mystery man - awaiting release in my mouth.

I collected all I had left, every shred of energy, and sucked and sucked until he was as far beyond control as I was. His cock spew semen down my throat, then slipped out of my tired lips, leaving a trail of goo on my chin. I swallowed all I could, but my body wouldn't cooperate, meaning I was helplessly sitting on the floor.

Everyone else was beyond done as well: hard male bodies surrounded me, half naked, with their softening cocks still sticking out of the flies of their jeans as they gasped for air, leaning against the toilet stall and tiled wall beyond.

There was only one who made the first move, Gary, who picked up the towel from the rack on the wall, and stepped towards me with that same proud grin on his face again that I'd seen the previous week after the game.

"There, love, let's get you cleaned up," he said.

I mustered an exhausted smile as I accepted the towel, but he refused to let it go, instead insisting on wiping the cum off my face and body for me.

He offered me his hand, allowing me to stand up precariously on my high heels, as I waited for my knees to start cooperating again.

We left the other three guys there, still gasping for air and unbelieving of their luck, while Gary led me inside the pub for some well-deserved refreshment.

Even if we'd stayed 'til closing, getting wasted out of our minds after that, I knew would remember that night. The night I was used at the pub.

BACKDOOR BEAUTY

———◆———

Gary and I had been dating a few months, and things were going very well between us. When he got home from work, he would give me that look, and before I knew it, I was spread against a wall, or bent over a table, with Gary shooting a load in me. I loved the attention.

Sex had always been an important part of my life, ever since that first time when I was still in my teens, but that's another story. This one deals with another first time. The one thing I could give Gary the pleasure of being the first to explore.

I'd done a lot before him, you see, I was insatiable, that's why we got on so well from the start. But I'd always felt that when you're really into someone, you ought to give them a gift of sorts. You have to give up something you've never given up before.

When I realised that Gary was the one, I knew, he'd be the first to fuck me in the ass. That was the one special thing I could offer him. Of course I knew he would gladly accept my gift.

When I first brought it up, I could tell from the look in his eye that he was interested. Not only that, he was chomping at the bit to get going. But he held back that night, he didn't go all the way.

"If we're going to do this, we're going to do this right," he said. "You'll let me have your virgin ass, and I'll ensure we do it in a way I've never done it before too."

My eyes lit up with the possibilities of what he was suggesting.

"What haven't you done before?" I asked.

"I've never taken a girl in public."

A smile formed on my lips and I was even more certain that we were meant to be.

I'd done it with people watching before, and knew I liked the attention. I wasn't shy about getting it on in public, as long as I was with the right guy. And of course, Gary was the right guy for everything.

And so we made a plan… The next weekend, we would go to the beach. Not just any beach, but a spot he'd heard about where people come to fuck in public. A dogging beach. I couldn't wait and spent most of the days leading up to it fantasising about it.

On the night in question, I'd spent much longer than normal getting ready. I made sure there wasn't a hair in sight; if my cunt and ass were going to be on display, I would make sure they were smooth and bare, like a pro. I imagined I was getting ready for a porn shoot, after all you never know if someone watching wants to capture the experience on film to view back later… In fact I was sort of hoping they would.

"Ready?" Gary called upstairs.

I smiled at my reflection in the mirror one last time. My lips were a perfect red, my ass looked perk-perfect in the short cut off jean shorts I chose for the occasion. Beach safe and smokin' hot. That's the look I was going for. A pair of black stiletto heels completed the look. If Gary was going to plunder my ass, I was going to make sure it looked it's absolute best.

"Coming!" I called out to him, while ruffling my brunette curls once more for volume. And off I went.

He drew in a sharp breath through his teeth. "You look amazing, Lolita."

I twirled once, wiggling my ass at him in the process. "You think?"

"Fuck yeah. I can't wait to get those shorts off you."

"Save your energy for when we get there," I turned, blowing a kiss at him when I faced him again.

I'd never seen Gary get in the car, start it up and pull out of the parking as quickly as that day. The beach was a bit of a drive away, allowing me the chance to warm up in the car. My hands found their way into Gary's lap and I felt that he was already pretty hard.

He groaned when I rubbed him through the thick denim of his jeans.

"Drive faster," I whispered, before nibbling on his ear lobe.

He did. He drove like the wind. What should have been a twenty minute drive, took us little more than ten. He parked up, whisked me out of the car by my hand and all but dragged me to a spot some ways between the beach and the parking. There were a few shrubs obscuring the view, and not much artificial light.

After a minute of letting my eyes adjust, the moonlight was sufficient to see the outline of some figures, standing around. There was a couple getting busy, and a group of individuals with glowing cigarettes in their hands watching. I couldn't make out from where I was, but I was pretty sure at least half of the watchers were pleasuring themselves as they observed the scene.

I'm not one to steal someone else's thunder, but Gary was determined not to waste any more time. He slapped my ass a couple of times, making me jump. The tingling burn felt amazing, and my cunt was already slick for him. But my cunt wasn't going to be the main attraction tonight!

Gary wrapped his arm around my waist and pressed his hard cock into my left ass cheek. He clearly didn't have any more patience left.

The couple nearby prepared for their final crescendo, their voices breaking the peaceful silence surrounding us. Those bystanders who hadn't yet finished turned to face us, eager to find further stimulation. I could feel their eyes burning into me, exciting me.

Gary unzipped himself, and pushed me down on my knees. I knew exactly what he wanted and took his length into my mouth eagerly. I let him face fuck me, taking his length as far as I could, deep into my throat. He groaned and gasped for air, then pulled back.

A quick check around us revealed that the watchers had stepped up closer around us. I thought that I could even see the couple who had just finished in the small crowd. Now that they had come closer I realised they were wearing masks, weird ones. Some looked almost like animals, or ancient gods as they stood silently in a semi-circle around our position.

Gary didn't take notice, or didn't care. He pulled me up on my feet again, ready for the second course. A blow job was always a sure fire way to get his engine going, though tonight he cut it short.

I took my shirt off, and posed in front of him just in my short shorts and bra, bending over deeply to give him a little glimpse of what was to come.

The bystanders sighed in appreciation, groping at themselves in the darkness. The scene made me want to please not just Gary, but them also. I wanted to be desired, objectified, admired. I wanted Gary to feel proud of me, showing me off to anyone who wanted to watch.

Behind me, Gary spanked me again, before rubbing his hand over the round part of my ass, then reaching downwards between my legs, all but setting my cunt on fire with anticipation.

I unbuttoned my shorts and wiggled out of the super tight shorts, letting them drop on the floor. I wasn't wearing anything underneath…

Gary breathed in through his teeth, then took a step in my direction again, his arm firmly hanging on to my waist. He slipped his cock into my pussy with ease, giving me a few hard thrusts until my moans became louder.

One of the bystanders blew a load into the grassy sand beside me. I wish it had actually hit me, but it seemed wrong to directly speak to them. The atmosphere was one of quiet understanding and anonymity. I felt like we were pushing the limits of what was acceptable by not wearing masks ourselves.

Gary slipped out of me so abruptly I felt like punching him. I wanted to be fucked, to be owned. I wanted these strangers to see what Gary could do. He was quite the stud, it's why I loved him.

But of course he was keen to proceed on, to claim his ultimate prize.

I bent down deeply for him, my tits threatened to spill out of my push-up bra. He placed his hand on top of my ass, kneading it in a circular motion with his thumb. Then with his other hand he explored my puckered anus, caressing it, massaging it to loosen me up. I was tight, so much so that it took him quite a bit of effort and lubrication to push his finger inside.

When he managed it I gasped in surprise. What a peculiar feeling! I was full, but not in the usual spot. It was a good kind of strange, his finger rubbing against my asshole, loosening it up just a little bit. He pulled it out and then returned with two fingers, wet with saliva probably, and working at my anus again to make their way inside.

I cried out when he forced them in. My ass burned a little, the muscles surrounding the entrance doing their best to expel his fingers again. But he didn't give in.

My hands rested on my thighs, as I tried to maintain balance. The sensations caused by his anal explorations were intense, almost overwhelming. I hadn't expected to feel this way.

In my mind, offering him my anal cherry was meant to be a surprise, a gift to him. But how I felt right now suggested it would be as much a gift for me as well. I would enjoy this, I knew it already. Two fingers weren't nearly as thick as Gary's cock, and the anticipation drove me wild with desire.

"More," I whispered, unable to bear the silence any longer. "Please."

Gary leant forward, his face just behind my neck. "Yes, my love." The rough tone in his voice gave me shivers. He couldn't wait, I knew that, but he was taking his time for me.

The gasps and groans, and the sound of flesh on flesh surrounding us signalled we were giving our audience a damn good show too.

I wiggled my ass backwards, into his hand, but he withdrew. Then I heard him spit, the wet saliva landing right in my crack. He spread it a little with his finger, before pressing something else, something bigger against my backdoor. His cock, at last.

The head of Gary's cock is quite a bit bigger than the shaft. Round and bulbous you might say. He pushed against me hard, and I did my best to relax. It hurt a little bit, the pressure became very intense, until I could feel it giving way.

The force with which he entered me was extreme, that's how hard he'd had to fight to make it past the outer ring of my anus. I cried out loudly when he made it inside, even he did.

He paused for a moment, as my ass was getting used to this new, much larger object inside. The burn I'd felt earlier with his fingers was nothing on what I felt now. It was like his cock was on fire inside me.

I shifted my weight from one foot to the other, finding the right angle, and then I was ready. He noticed the change in me immediately and started to move. Slowly and carefully he pulled out some of the way, taking care not to let it be forced out. Then he pushed back, firmly but slowly. I gasped for air when he managed to fill me entirely.

And then again, he withdrew, before thrusting it back inside. I was breathless, almost dizzy and overcome by sensations I'd never known before.

Despite there being no direct stimulation to my cunt, it started dripping again. I was desperate to be fucked harder and deeper, but I kept quiet and let him set the pace.

This was for him. My gift for Gary.

He soon found his rhythm, each movement coming faster than the previous. His fingers dug hard into my hips to keep me steady, and soon he was banging me almost as normal. The big difference was the tightness. Despite how fast he was going, and how much he'd fucked me already, my ass continued to grip him in a stranglehold. I was surprise he'd lasted as long as he had already.

Several of the masked strangers surrounding us had been forced to finish by our spectacle. I wasn't in any position to see much, the intensity of Gary's thrusts forced my eyes shut. But the sounds of guys jerking themselves off to muffled groans and grunts reduced, until there were just a couple left.

I was desperate for release by this point, gagging for it. Gary noticed my predicament and reached around, tending to my clit while he continuously ploughed into my ass. It was glorious. His fingers knew just how to soothe me, whip me into a frenzy and tease me back down again.

He toyed with me, getting me close to the edge of orgasm, then paused, leaving me hanging. It was painful and glorious all at once.

I decided to play along, tightening up further as much as I could, until the pressure on his cock was so strong, he could no longer ignore it. I felt invigorated, back in charge and opened my eyes.

Next to me, one of the quiet strangers held something in his hand, a light shone straight into my eyes. A camera. I smiled to myself, my fantasy had come true.

This triumphant moment was going to be recorded in history, even if just on some random guy's phone. I hoped he would upload it somewhere, so someday we might come across it randomly. A reminder of how I gave my ass to Gary.

Behind me, Gary was getting close, I could tell by the way his breathing had changed. He was panting, and each thrust was accompanied by a low growl. I closed my eyes again, focusing on standing my ground against the force of his movements. When he came, the feeling of relief was overwhelming. The hot gushing liquid soothed my burning skin, and made it tingle even more at the same time. He pulled out and some of it spilled out of my ass with him.

It was unusual, so different from getting creamed in the cunt. I felt properly loosened up, like nothing could ever make it tight again. The gushing semen was a clear signal that the loose feeling wasn't just in my head.

Gary reached around to my clit again, tweaking and manipulating it like he knew I enjoyed. I was still on edge, after being so horny for so long. He pushed his semi-erect member against my cunt from the back. It felt delicious, though not quite enough to finish me off.

His other hand found my tits, squeezing them and tweaking my nipples one after the other. I took a deep breath and focused on his movements. There was nothing left in this world but him, me, and my growing pleasure.

He must have done the same thing, because only

moments later, just when I was starting to get there, he pushed his cock into my pussy and immediately went at it with an intensity that made my eyes water.

There he was, my Gary, the man who could make me weak with only a look. He fucked me hard, spending what little energy he had regained during the short break on getting me over the edge.

His cock was just hard enough, the angle just right, his fingers gentle enough as he brought me closer and closer to the finish line. I cried out, staring straight into the lens of that one stranger's camera phone, as all the pent up tension inside me erupted into an orgasm so glorious, I wondered if I'd ever have another one like it.

My knees were shaking, and Gary's arm around my waist was the only thing holding me up, as I continued to ride the wave of pleasure he'd caused. I was utterly spent, but he continued to hold me from behind, littering my bare shoulder with kisses.

Even after the bystanders dissipated, having had their fill of our bareback action, we still stood there, in the same place.

"That was… wow," I finally said.

He chuckled. "It's all you. I just came along for the ride."

He released me and let his cock slip out, before pulling

his jeans back up. I searched around in the sand for my shirt, and put my shorts back on as well. My footing was still unsteady as I started to walk back towards the car. He paused, picked me up into his arms and carried me all the way back.

"Love you, Gary," I whispered.

"I love you too."

DEFLOWERED

This is a story from a long time ago, from a time when I was just starting to discover my sexuality. At eighteen years old, I was a little late to the party compared to others I hung out with. Of course you'd never know it if you looked at me, no, I developed quite early on and the boys had certainly noticed. But I'd never gotten close to any of them.

You see, I had specific ideas of who I wanted to give my virginity to. He should be handsome, sexy - all those are a given. But I had set my sights on a mature partner, one who would be experienced enough not to fumble in the dark and give me the pleasure I'd craved.

I'd set my sights on a man, rather than a boy.

His name was Mr. Blakely- we affectionately called him Blake.

Blake was a substitute teacher at my school. Although I'd only been in his class a couple of times when our English teacher, Mr. Argyle was off sick, I knew he was the one from the moment I laid eyes on him.

I wasn't after romance, not at all, just an experience. A one time, very special experience that I would remember forever.

It all began at the graduation dance…

My friends and I of course had been drinking beforehand. After all, you don't graduate every day, so the occasion was worthy of a grand celebration! None of them were virgins, except Mary, whose catholic upbringing had held her back so far.

On this very last night as High School students, even her patience had worn thin.

We made a pact. We would both try to seduce Blake, and his choice would be final. Our other friends even bet on who would win. As soon as the rules were established (no roofies), we were ready to make our respective moves on poor, unsuspecting Blake who had supervision duties at the dance.

"May the best girl win," I whispered in Mary's ear, without letting my mark out of my sight for more than a second.

She nodded at me with a naughty smile and cut through the dancing crowd towards my right, until she was a couple of steps ahead of me. I rushed into action, unwilling to be left behind, even if I felt confident that even if she got there first, Blake would pick me in a heartbeat. I wouldn't give him any other choice.

"So…" Mary started, as soon as she came face-to-face

with her victim.

"So…" he responded, eyeing her as she twirled a lock of hair around her index finger.

What a rookie move!

"Enjoying the dance?" she asked, and I felt like face-palming myself.

He was a teacher, not a student, why would *he* enjoy the dance when he wasn't going to do any dancing?

"It's all right."

"Blake… " I said, in my most sultry voice.

"Yes, Lolita?"

"I think what Mary is trying to say is that you could enjoy the dance much more than what you are now."

"How so?" Blake's eyes met my own and I felt a surge of excitement as well as nerves. What if he wouldn't go for it? Rejection would be so embarrassing.

"Well, a few of us are going to head upstairs for some…" I'd wanted to say *privacy*, but figured it was too early for that. "Peace and quiet."

"The classrooms are off limits, you know that."

"Yeah, we know, but you see now that we've graduated, we're really not going to be seeing those anymore. So it's kind of a goodbye. You wouldn't refuse us our goodbye, would you, Blake?" I blinked innocently at him, seeing his expression soften slightly. No, he wouldn't stand in our way.

"So. Upstairs, you say? And then?" Blake asked.

"There's a bottle of wine in my locker, in case we get, you know… Thirsty." I emphasised every letter of the word, trying to gauge his reaction.

"Right, and it would be awesome if you could join us. For one last goodbye," Mary interjected, resting his hand on Blake's upper arm.

He twitched slightly at her touch, but I noticed anyway. Jesus, she's really going for it!

Looking at Mary, dressed up in a tight, black mini dress, she looked a lot less catholic than her parents would have liked. She looked fucking hot.

"Pretty please?" I plead, while trying to regain Blake's full attention.

His eyes crossed mine, and I the glimmer of a smile appeared on his lips as he looked back and forth between Mary and I. That's when I understood that this contest of ours was going to fail, unless we changed the rules…

Moments later, while our friends watched from across the room, exchanging remarks and speculating on the outcome of our little wager, Mary and I managed to convince Blake to join us in Room 101. We were to head up first, concealing the bottle in my coat, and he would follow as soon as he could slip away unnoticed.

"Hey, Mary," I whispered as we walked up the broad stairs leading to the classrooms on the first floor.

"Yeah. Wow, can you believe he's actually meeting us upstairs? I think he likes me."

"Mary, focus!" I paused for a moment, waiting for her to look at me properly. "We're going to have to change things up."

"Aw, man! You're just saying that because he likes me better."

I shook my head. Jesus, she could be thick sometimes.

"No, I think he likes both of us. We're going to have to make him an offer he can't refuse."

Mary stopped at the top of the stairs and turned to face me. "What are you saying?"

"We're going to have to let him do us both. Together."

Her mouth fell wide open as she continued to stare at me. "A threesome? You, me, and Blake?"

There was a moment of silence between us, and I worried that her pride was going to get in the way of this brilliant idea. Surely she had to see that it was the only sure-fire way that we'd get in his pants that night.

"Not how I imagined my first time... " Mary mumbled. "But... " A devious smile appears on her lips.

Yes! She was in.

"OK, so here's the plan. How about we stand lookout,

and when we hear Blake coming up the stairs, we start making out as if we don't realise he's coming."

Mary grinned at me, before obviously checking me out head to toe. "That's easy. Nothing we haven't done before…"

"Trust me, he won't be able to resist!" I clapped my hands with excitement. He wouldn't know what hit him. It would be glorious.

No sooner did we finish discussing the plan, and stepped inside the classroom, did we hear footsteps coming up the stairs. We were on. It was time.

Mary practically jumped me, wrapping her arms around my neck and pressing her lips tightly against mine. I rested my hands on her hips, ready to go for more of a feel as soon as Blake arrived.

Her lips were sweet, tasting of cherry lip gloss mixed with the Bacardi Breezer she'd had earlier. She was right, this wasn't anything we hadn't already done, though in the past it had been more of a laugh, an experiment to see what it would be like to touch another girl. Now, things were a lot more serious.

The door opened and from the corner of my eye I could see Blake frozen in the entrance. His eyes were fixed on us, as we continued to play, tasting each other, with our bodies pressed tightly against one another.

He didn't say a word, I could only hear the sharp intake of breath which was barely louder than the hammering beat of my own heart. Well, if he wasn't leaving, that meant most the battle was already won.

I let my hand wander from her hips upwards over Mary's side, then back and down again until my palm rested squarely on her ass cheek. She was curvy in all the right places, and I had to admit it was a turn on.

What was even more of a turn on was Blake's silhouette, quietly observing our every move.

Mary moaned into my lips, prompting me to grab her ass harder, pulling her backwards with me until I was able to clamber onto the teacher's desk behind me. I sat, spread my legs, and pulled her against me again.

Meanwhile she began exploring me by touch as well, running her fingertips over my neckline; the fabric of my dress at first, but then she started softly caressing my bare skin just above. It tickled, pleasantly so, making me return her earlier moan. Our lips never stopped touching.

Time seemed to stand still as we continued to take each other higher and higher into the realms of lust, with Blake watching us do our thing. Finally, he snapped out of his trance and shut the door behind himself.

With difficulty, I tore myself away from Mary's feverish kisses, and looked him in the eye.

"Hi, Blake," I whispered. "Ready for this dance to get a whole lot better?"

He didn't reply, but as his hand travelled downwards, reaching the button on his jeans, I knew we'd both won. Soon, we'd get our reward.

Mary looked back as well, her eyes fixed on his movements as he unzipped himself and let his right hand slip inside his boxers. When she turned to face me again, she couldn't stop grinning.

I cupped her face in my hands before kissing her once more, deeper than before, and looking into her brown eyes. Time to involve Blake. She nodded, and let go of me, instead walking up to Blake with her hand stretched out, inviting him to approach us.

"You're not just going to watch, are you?" she asked.

Blake bit his bottom lip and let his eyes wander over the both of us. I quickly realised the problem: we were still dressed.

"Mary," I said, while turning around, facing away from them both. "Unzip me?"

The approaching footsteps behind me told me that she was coming back. But it wasn't her hand that ended up resting on my back, it was bigger... I looked back to find Blake towering over me, his fingers fumbling with the zip of my dress until it came down all the way, exposing my naked, bra-less back and the top of the thong I'd chosen to wear.

Mary joined us as well, running her fingertips over my freshly exposed skin, tempting him further.

I turned around, with my dress just about clinging on to the top of my shoulders, before letting it fall down onto the floor. I knew I was pretty, but the way Blake looked at me stirred up a new, hotter fire inside the pit of my stomach. His tense expression suggested he was one step away from devouring me.

I smiled, and looked down coyly at my bare tits, then back at him.

His boxers were tenting severely, it was even more obvious since he'd removed his hand from there. *Soon. Soon I would find out what a cock feels like.* At the time I had no idea it would be the beginning of an obsession of a lifetime.

"Tell me what to do," I whispered, when he got near me.

The look he gave me suggested he knew then that this wasn't just any fuck for me, but my first one.

He took my hand and placed it on top of his cock. It felt so hard through the cotton fabric. So thick…

I explored his length as best I could, but it was difficult with his underwear in the way. A deep breath and sudden surge in confidence later, I slipped my hand inside. He felt warm, no, hot. It was as if I could feel all the blood that had rushed into his erection through the silkiness of his skin. Throbbing, pulsating, readying itself for what was about to occur.

Mary stood off to the side a little bit, struggling with the side zip of her dress until it finally let go. Soon, she was equally naked, and quite a sight to behold.

Blonde curls crowned her virgin pussy, which she gently caressed before slipping a finger inside. All the while, her eyes were fixed on Blake and me, as I started to jerk him off.

I wasn't sure what was more arousing: what I was doing, or the fact that Mary was watching me. It was such a thrill to share this moment with her. Our combined anticipation made things very special indeed.

Blake rested his hand on top of mine, guiding my movements, the amount of pressure I put on his cock, as well as the rhythm. It must have been obvious that I wasn't experienced, though I was very eager to learn to please.

Mary stumbled backwards on top of the desk I had sat on before and spread wide, allowing herself better access. She started flicking her clit, moaning with every move. I let go of Blake, eager to give him more of a show before the main course could begin.

As well as heighten his pleasure, I wanted to increase my own anticipation by stretching the moment a little longer.

I fell onto my knees in front of the desk, making sure Mary's legs rested on either one of my shoulders. Then, I burrowed my face deeply into her folds without hesitation.

She cried out, surprised, but then fell back onto the table again, writhing her hips, forcing my tongue deeply inside her. Her sweet, salty taste remains a vivid memory to this day.

Blake stepped up next to Mary, grabbed her hair and pressed his lips against hers as she continued to moan. I watched as he kissed her, then released her again and placed his lips on her nipple.

She was fighting it a bit, spasming involuntarily as we continued to stimulate her. Her cries grew louder and louder, and I tried my best to keep up, licking her slit with as much enthusiasm as I'd hoped someone would show for me later.

"Oh yeah!" she screamed. "That's it!"

I stuck my tongue in her as far as it would go, and rubbed her clit with my thumb at the same time. She shook violently against the table, her hair flying wildly as she shivered and shuddered until she was completely sated.

I pulled back and found Blake staring at me. His eyes - much darker than normal - bore into me, a clear indicator of how thin his self-control had worn throughout Mary's orgasm.

He wanted me, I could tell, and I was desperate for his attention.

Leaving Mary to regain her strength, I walked over to another table, and sat on top, keeping my legs spread wide. I didn't even need to beckon him over, because he was already right there in front of me.

"Have you ever had a virgin before?" I whispered in his ear.

His after-shave was intoxicating. He smelled manly, musky, yet clean. Hard to explain.

He didn't answer, just positioned himself between my legs. A man on a mission: he knew exactly what he wanted.

"It won't hurt… too much," he said, as he rubbed his cock against my swollen folds.

So good, so gentle yet firm. Just that was almost enough to get me off, but I bit my lip and tried to focus on lasting just a little bit longer.

He pressed against me, struggling against my tight pussy, which refused to let him in at first. *Was he too big? Would I miss out on my first fuck because he couldn't fit it in?*

"Relax," he said through gritted teeth, while spreading

me further with his thumb and forefinger.

I closed my eyes and tried to breathe deeply. In and out.

Then with an intense sting and burn, he was in.

My foreplay with Mary had made me wet, sure, but he was so big that it was painful to move at first. He paused for a moment, while I tried to decide if this had in fact been a terrible idea.

He wasn't even wearing a condom!

But then, my insides relaxed, and with it, my doubts vanished.

He started to slip in and out more easily as my juices lubricated the both of us. I went from pain to pleasure within seconds, a fact I couldn't keep to myself. I moaned as he thrust deeply into me, gasped when he withdrew.

My breaths quickened, until I felt faint. But still, I didn't want it to stop.

When I opened my eyes, I could see Blake's face, strained into a frown, with droplets of sweat collecting on his forehead. At this rate, he wouldn't last too long either, I could feel it.

Behind him, Mary got up off the table and sashayed over to us. Her eyes were drunk with pleasure, clearly that oral orgasm wasn't going to satisfy her. She wanted a bit of the action I was getting too.

"My turn," she said, bending forward over the table, presenting her perfectly formed, round ass to Blake and me.

I reached over, feeling the curve of her buttocks. Soft, tempting skin, slipping past my fingertips. Poor Blake didn't know where to look. At my tits, bouncing up and down as he continued to fuck me, my mouth, which he knew was capable of immense pleasure, at least when used on a girl's cunt, or Mary's ass.

Always the fair one, Blake pulled out of me, and aimed his impressive cock at Mary's pussy. He was already slick with my nectar, and as a result, managed to enter her with a lot more ease. *Dirty girl, perhaps she wasn't a virgin after all!*

Mary yelped as he rammed into her balls deep, then turned to look at Blake. He pushed her back down onto the table, and started giving her a good fuck. Clearly, she wasn't as tight as me, or else he would have started off easy. She'd never admitted it, but at that point I was certain Mary had had a cock before. If not a real one, then at the very least a toy.

I considered my options. On the one hand, I was so goddamn horny that all I really wanted was to finish myself off, but on the other, I couldn't let the opportunity slip past to have a bit more fun with Blake and Mary.

I knelt down again, right next to Mary's left thigh, and

looked up expectantly at Blake. *What would cock taste like*, I wondered. Considering he'd been fucking first me, and now Mary, I figured it would be pretty much the same as pussy. What cock tasted of au naturel was something I would have to discover on my own, later.

He pulled out of Mary as abruptly as he had done to me earlier, and eagerly pushed his thick man sausage into my mouth. I tried my best to accommodate him, but I again had to deal with the fact that he was absolutely huge. I licked his head, which he seemed to really enjoy, then sucked him harder and harder, until he was all but incapacitated.

"Enough," he grunted, and took his impossibly thick and long manhood away from me again in order to thrust it back into Mary's dripping cunt.

Then he took my hand to help me get up and motioned over towards Mary.

"Get on top of her."

I looked at her angelic face, her dark blonde hair fanned out over the desk as her boobs shook with every push of his hips. She was hot. Hell yes, I could get on top of that!

I got up on all fours beside her, then spread and lowered myself on top of her naked body.

The second I was in place, I felt something wet push

against my aching pussy.

Blake was going to do us in turns, right there on top of each other!

He thrust into me, and I dove down for a mouthful of boob.

Mary cried out and forced her hand in between us for more manual stimulation. Her fingers brushed past my nipples, which had become sore, they were so hard. It was beautiful, as well as frustrating.

I took her other hand and guided it up towards my chest, and soon enough she was rubbing herself as well as my tits, while Blake continued to stretch me out from behind.

I gasped and cried out, so painfully close to release I couldn't stand it any longer. I ground down, trying to get my clit close to Mary's fingers, just to give me that extra push I needed.

Then, as I reached new heights, a finger ventured somewhere entirely unexpected.

I looked back to find Blake - a man obsessed - feeling his way around my spread ass. It wasn't something I had thought about or considered trying before, but his enthusiasm swayed me.

He pushed against my puckered anus with his thumb, stretching it similarly to how his cock had done to my pussy earlier.

I moaned, then I cried, then I muffled a loud scream as he forced it inside, filling me from two holes at once and way beyond my capacity. At that moment, my orgasm washed over me. I was overwhelmed, incapacitated, and completely and utterly lost.

My muscles twitched and shuddered to a halt, I could no longer move. Blake tried to continue but in the midst of my spasms, I felt him erupt inside me as well.

Our bodies ground to a halt, unable to do anything except ride the wave of pleasure he'd unleashed upon me. Mary, helpless underneath, feverishly rubbed herself to a similar ending. It was amazing, we were reduced to a sweaty mass of bodies, unwilling to move ourselves out of the compromising position we'd found ourselves in.

I idly wondered, what if we got caught? They could do nothing to us, but Blake would probably lose his job. But this thought remained just that: an irrelevant concern that never came to pass.

When I finally regained the strength to get up, I found that Blake had slipped away at some point without either Mary or me noticing. He must have been equally worried someone would find out. He was supposed to be supervising the dance downstairs after all.

Mary seemed to have no worry in the world; she

looked like she'd been drugged. Probably had a bit much to drink in an effort to gain some Dutch courage and it was finally catching up…

Meanwhile I was on top of the world, only brought back into reality when I noticed how sore my knees were. Whether they'd been bruised when I was kneeling on the ground in front of Mary or Blake, or later, on top of the table, I wasn't sure.

I wasn't sure of a lot of things at that moment, like what it meant that I'd been so turned on making out with Mary before. But one thing was certain: from the moment my cherry got popped, I had realised I really loved cock. And I vowed that the next one I had one, I wouldn't share the attention with anyone else.

If anything, perhaps I should try having sex with two guys at once, that way I could be the centre of attention. Yes, that seemed like a very tempting idea… One I could get used to.

GETTING A RAISE

I've never been a career oriented person. It had been three years since I'd been working as a receptionist at the corporate HQ of a large car parts manufacturer. Putting through phone calls, receiving visitors, that kind of thing.

It was easy work, and I enjoyed it. I especially enjoyed getting dressed up before a big meeting, when I knew a lot of visitors would come in. Frazzled looking businessmen, in town just for a day or so, their jetlagged eyes would almost light up when they saw me sitting at the reception desk.

The attention made the job rewarding for me. They enjoyed the eye candy, I enjoyed seeing their reactions.

Things were chugging along just fine at this pace until Gary and I started to make big future plans. We were going to buy a house together. We'd even already found one we had our eyes on, but there was an obstacle in our way. There was no way the bank would lend us enough money, unless we could increase our combined monthly income somehow. Gary's job had no scope for a raise, so any extra money would have to come in from me.

So we hatched a plan…

It was the last Friday of the month, and I'd dressed myself with even more care than usually that day. A very well fitted black suit, with a pencil skirt so tight you could actually see the outline of my stocking tops through the soft fabric if you paid attention.

In all our adventures, Gary and I had one rule that was never to be broken: any time I'm getting involved with other people, he has to know about it and be there, even if he's not participating. So he'd taken a half day off, arriving at the back entrance of the office just towards the end of lunch time. I snuck him inside, into the attached closet of the boardroom, ready for whatever was going to go down later.

Like at every month end, the three partners, Mr. Black, Mr. Murdoch and Mr. Lewis had planned a meeting that was to last all afternoon. They'd go through the figures, analysing what had worked and what needed improving in the business.

The three of them were very hands-on in their business, as most self-made men tend to be. Although the company was successful enough, and had turned the three of them into billionaires, still they worked as hard, if not harder than anyone else at the office.

They also had a weak spot for me, the pretty receptionist twenty years their junior. The not-quite-covert looks in my direction on various occasions had made that very clear, though they'd never acted forward with me, hanging on to the illusion of their broken marriages, possibly out of habit.

So we were all set. Three sexually frustrated middle aged rich guys, one receptionist with great ambition, and a husband in the closet, keeping a video camera at the ready.

"Lolita," Mr. Black's voice came through the intercom.

"Yes, Mr. Black?" I answered.

"We are ready for our monthly meeting. Would you be so kind and hold our phone calls until we're done."

"Sure thing, Mr. Black." I smiled to myself, enjoying the sudden surge of excitement that coursed through my whole body. It was time.

The reception area was quiet, as it always was on the last Friday of the month. Most of the office had left at lunchtime for their half day off, so it was just me and the new girl, Cassie, manning the desk. We didn't expect any visitors, but I was confident she could manage on her own.

"Cover for me, Cass?" I asked.

She looked up, nail file still in hand and nodded.

"I'll be a little while, I need to make an important phone call."

She shrugged, then continued to fix her nails as if my presence made very little difference to her. Obviously she was just counting down the minutes until five o'clock, and I couldn't blame her.

With a spring in my step, I made my way through the corridor leading towards the board room, picking up the refreshments trolley on the way. That was to be my cover: coffee, tea and biscuits for the partners. With a side of pussy.

Knock, knock.

"Enter," Mr. Lewis's voice filtered through the heavy wooden door.

I stuck my head in first, leaning forward to give them a bit of cleavage view as I entered the room.

"Coffee, tea?" I asked, smiling widely at the three of them, who looked a bit worse for wear after what must have been a tiring week.

"Thanks, darling. Don't mind if I do," Mr. Murdoch - always the most forward of the three - answered.

I poured him a coffee, black, no sugar, just as I knew he liked.

The other two sat back and observed me, leaning over the table to push the cup towards Mr. Murdoch, while giving them a good view of everything on offer.

"I think I'll have a cup of tea, if you don't mind," Mr. Black said, his voice sounding distant.

I smiled at him and nodded, pouring the tea.

"There you go." I slid the cup towards him, leaning forward way further than strictly necessary. His eyes were helplessly drawn into the depths of my cleavage. The deep cut of my suit jacket couldn't disguise the lack of blouse underneath.

He caught himself after a moment of silence, blushing as he accepted the cup and looked away.

"And for you, Mr. Lewis?" I asked with my head cocked.

"Umm… are those chocolate chip cookies?" He pointed towards the lower level of the trolley.

I nodded, of course. Mr. Lewis and the never-ending diet his wife had put him on. He wouldn't be able to resist the cookies.

"A coffee then, to go with those cookies."

I turned around and bent down deeply to retrieve the plate of cookies for him, before pouring his coffee. The strain on the tight skirt was immense, and I was certain all three of them couldn't stop themselves from looking. I could feel it.

"Say, Mr. Murdoch," I said, after placing the cookies and coffee in front of Mr. Lewis with a bright smile.

"Yes, dear?" His eyes were on me, unapologetically so. Although getting on in age, he's always been the most alpha of the three of them.

"I know it's not the best timing, but I did have something I wanted to discuss with you. An HR related matter."

He raised an eyebrow, and a quick scan around the large mahogany table revealed the other two partners were paying equal attention to my words.

"I've been with you for three years now…" I started, quasi-nervously playing with a lock of my hair as I spoke.

"Yes…" Mr. Murdoch said.

"And I think I've proven to be reliable…" I let my voice trail off, while staring straight into Mr. Murdoch's eyes.

There's something there, a fire, a barely disguised desire. I know that look on a man better than anything.

"That's right. You've been an asset to the company."

"I was just wondering if perhaps there was something I could do, some extra responsibilities perhaps… " I lean forward slightly again, resting my palm on the table just next to his hand.

"In some way that was mutually beneficial…"

He stares back at me, making eye contact, then looking down at my red painted lips, finally lingering on my cleavage. I decide it's time. I caress his hand lightly with my pinkie finger, while continuing to look him in the eye.

Then I straighten myself, and look at the other two

partners. Mr. Black, who has developed a light sweat on his brow, and Mr. Lewis, who had already picked up a cookie, but has abandoned it after only one bite.

"I mean to say, if it pleases the three of you. I feel I have a lot more to offer than just taking phone calls." My last statement comes out a lot breathier than it was meant to, but the collection of hungry eyes, and half-open lips in my audience suggest that I've had the desired effect.

"I... " Mr. Murdoch stutters. Although he's always been the one of the the three with the biggest mouth, calling the female employees *darling,* and *sweetheart,* and whatnot, it seems I've rendered him speechless.

I look over at Mr. Lewis, whose receding hairline and out of shape physique don't quite disguise that just a few years ago he would've been quite the looker. He's fixed in place and still holding on to that half eaten chocolate chip cookie, not knowing quite what to do with himself.

In one swift move, I push myself up on the table next to Mr. Murdoch, and cross my legs. The move has made my skirt ride up high enough to reveal the lower edge of the lace stocking tops, which Mr. Murdoch is now helplessly staring at.

I fold my hands together on top of my knee, making no attempt to adjust my skirt back down.

"Dear, I'm not sure we're understanding you," Mr.

Black stammers behind me.

I lean back, resting on one hand and look him in the eye, which seems to make him even more nervous.

"Well, all I'm saying is, if there's *anything* I could do to please you… Above and beyond my regular job." The emphasis on *anything* should clear up the remaining doubts they have.

All three of them still look to be in shock, but everything from the looks in their eyes, to their rushed breaths and nervous fidgeting with their hands suggest they know where I'm going with this, and they're almost on the same page.

I think it's time to take things further.

With my other hand, I run my fingers down the side of my neck and into my cleavage, while maintaining eye contact with Mr. Black at first, then Mr. Lewis, who starts to cough nervously, and finally, Mr. Murdoch, who has leant back into his chair and seems to be enjoying the show the most right now.

"I think I understand," Mr. Murdoch says at last. "Before we go on, let's fix the terms."

I shoot him a naughty smile and nod. "Nothing outrageous, a little raise is all I need." I stare down at his crotch, amused by the double meaning of my demand.

A smile starts to form on his lips as he gets more

comfortable in his chair, his legs leisurely spread, revealing the beginnings of said *raise*, straining against his zip.

I bite my lower lip, excited about what's about to unfold.

"Just one more thing, and I do hope you won't mind…" I get up and slip off the table, kneeling in front of Mr. Murdoch and his ever growing erection.

"Sure, darling, what's that?" He groans as I place my hand on his crotch, feeling the hardness of his cock through the fabric of his suit trouser.

"I hope it's OK if someone gets to watch us…" I look up through my thick lashes at him, knowing that with every movement of my hand, he's less and less likely to refuse me anything I ask for.

"Sure, as it is, we've already got an audience here!" Mr. Murdoch gestures at the other two partners, who stare at us red-faced and visibly horny. I wonder when is the last time they ever even had sex last. Having met their respective wives, I can't imagine they give it up at all. A shame, letting these men languish in frustration, as they spend all their money and do nothing but nag.

It's a situation I intend to put an end to single-handedly right now.

"You can come in now," I shout, and immediately the closet door opens to reveal Gary, who looks at least as hot and bothered as Mr. Murdoch whose cock is in my hand.

The other two let out surprised gasps, but don't protest, as Gary makes his way around the table towards the other side of the board room to get a better look at me on my knees.

I unzip Mr. Murdoch, freeing his aching erection from the confines of his trousers, and wet my lips in anticipation. He cries out and grabs a fistful of hair as I let his cock into my mouth and start to suck it enthusiastically.

These are the groans of a man who's not had a good sucking in a long while…

Beside us, I hear another zip open up, and I look over to find Mr. Lewis, who's put his half-eaten cookie down onto the table, grabbing hold of his cock hard. His face has turned all red and sweaty while he gets himself ready.

I've never been with a fat guy before, but the prospect is fascinating. I'm all about the new experiences.

Mr. Black I assume is also pleasuring himself now, as the sounds behind me seem to suggest. Meanwhile Gary has turned on the camera and is moving around me, getting a close up of my lips around Murdoch's thick, veiny cock.

I can't take the tension any longer and let my hands travel between my thighs, where the pushed up skirt is barely concealing my naked cunt. Well prepared as always,

I had taken off my panties at lunchtime to prepare for this meeting. My slick slit awaited my touch eagerly, it was a relief when my fingers finally made their way between my folds to find my clit.

I moaned into Murdoch's cock, sucking on it hungrily. Behind me, a chair screeched against the wooden floor, followed by reluctant footsteps.

Looking up from the expert sucking I was giving Murdoch, I saw Mr. Black approach with his hands down his pants, fapping furiously. I got up, leaving Mr. Murdoch in agony as I unzipped the side of my skirt, wiggling my ass to free myself from its skin tight fabric.

I opened the buttons on my jacket, revealing a lusciously filled black lace bra which matched the garter belt holding up the stockings perfectly.

Gary moved around us, camera in one hand, cock in the other, getting the best view of the upcoming action. I positioned myself chest down on the board room table, my ass presented to both Mr. Black and Mr. Murdoch who were behind me, trying to decide who got to go first. In front of me sat the cookie plate, behind it Mr. Lewis, who could not take his eyes off me. I picked up a cookie, and licked it, all the while maintaining eye contact with him.

He groaned, and tightened his grip on his swollen member, speeding up.

"Come on, gimme a taste," I whispered.

He didn't need telling twice and struggled out of his chair, while fumbling with his trousers to make them drop down all the way.

Behind me, someone's cock was impatiently nudging at my entrance, making me squeal with delight. Almost… I was almost exactly where I wanted to be.

Then he slammed into me, burrowing himself into my wet cunt balls deep, making me scream out into Mr. Lewis's pre-cum lathered head. I forced my body to relax, taking the impatient fuck from behind, while opening my mouth and throat wide for the cock waiting in front of my lips.

Mr. Lewis grabbed a handful of hair, and firmly entered my mouth. He was surprisingly thick, as well as long. He groaned loudly as he pushed against the tight ring of my throat, desperate for me to swallow his entire length. His hands were trembling, his expression one of the most urgent need I've ever seen. God, did it turn me on.

I didn't mind his hand pushing my head down, or his cock almost blocking my windpipe. He seemed to be almost in pain, and the only thing that would soothe him was this blowjob. The poor guy, I was certain he was in this much of a state due to the worst case of blue balls ever recorded.

I sucked and sucked, as one of the others behind me grabbed hold of my hips hard and continued to fuck me wide. I could do this. Please all three of them until they were completely satisfied. I'd had more at once before, but never anyone in this much need.

As I started to speed up, encouraged by Mr. Lewis's relaxing expression, I reached for him, unbuttoning his shirt, until I could slip my hand inside, caressing flesh which had probably not felt much affection for quite some time. He opened his eyes, almost in surprise, as I reached around, holding on to his love-handles to get some control over the rhythm of what had turned from slow and hard into a fast and shallow blow job.

He had turned increasingly flushed, sticky with sweat, but still very much caught up in the moment. Just when I thought he'd reached the point of no return, did his face find focus again and he pulled out of me, leaving me helplessly waiting. I leant up on my elbows, waiting to see what he was up to, when he sprayed my face with his hot load.

Oh my god, the amount of cum this man had produced was amazing. Clearly, he'd been saving it up just for this moment.

I did my best to swallow, lick up anything that dribbled down my lips. It was hopeless though, the entire bottom half of my face was coated in his man juices, as he continued to jerk the last drops out of his cock.

"You've had your fun," a voice - sounding like a much more primal, wilder version of Mr. Black, said behind me. "The ass is mine."

In the resulting commotion, two pairs of hands picked me up and flipped me onto my side, my cheek landing right in the centre of a puddle of cum on top of the table. That's when the fingers started to probe, discover, examine how best to take my remaining orifice.

Mr. Lewis sat back down on his chair, and picked up the cookie I had licked earlier, eating it one little bite at a time as he watched the remaining commotion at the other end of the table.

I lifted my head, following his line of sight until I saw Mr. Murdoch and Mr. Black, almost elbowing each other out of the way to get to me.

Why take turns? I thought, *when both can do what they like to me at the same time...*

I raised my legs towards my face until I was in a foetal position on top of the table. The men understood when I slipped my hand down between my legs and spread my lips to present my cunt to them, while my ass was obviously on display at the same time.

They angled themselves accordingly, two cocks

pointing in my direction next to each other, and again I found myself with two pairs of hands keeping me in place.

It was Mr. Black who entered me first this time, forcing his thick cock between my ass cheeks and into the depths of my anus. I cried out with the shock of it, and my surprise almost instantly turned into pure pleasure.

My pleasure was heightened when Mr. Murdoch slipped his trouser snake back into my pussy. They fumbled around a little bit, until they found their rhythm, holding on to me tightly, and fucking me at the same speed and intensity.

It was intense, being ravished by two men at once. Two strong, mature, powerful men, who clearly worked very well together, both in a professional setting as well as one this intimate.

They fucked me, faster and faster, their gasping breaths getting louder as their speed increased. I was getting ever closer, with every push of their double penetration forcing me towards my sweet, long awaited release.

I don't know how long it went on for, I just remember feeling high. Almost like I was floating, instead of lying on a table. I squeezed my thighs together, tightening my cunt for Mr. Murdoch, who groaned to a halt, emptying his balls into my depths.

With it, Mr. Black's final thrust pushed him into a

glorious, spasming orgasm.

Feeling the two of them fill me simultaneously was all I needed to go off myself. My cries echoed off the board room walls, as the immense pleasure from our illicit pursuits overwhelmed me.

I shuddered and shivered against the table, not knowing where to put my hands - settling on grabbing a handful of boob with one, and using the other to rub my clit to keep my pleasure going longer.

When I calmed myself, felt every muscle which had only just been frozen in position relax a bit, I noticed the three men continued to watch. The fourth man - my man, Gary - stepped up, handing the video camera to Mr. Murdoch, who didn't question it, just continued to point it at us.

I could tell he was very close to release himself, Gary's expression, which I had become so familiar with in the time we'd been together told me that. He tugged at himself, teasing himself, looking me right in the eye as he edged himself closer to orgasm.

Knowing he liked to watch, I continued to play with my tits, spread my legs to give him a good view of what my fingers were doing down there too, and waited.

"Cum for me, baby," I mouthed, hardly any sound passing over my lips I was that exhausted.

He did, spraying my tits with his white sticky mess, as he let out one final, ultimate groan.

I smiled at him when he opened his eyes again. I was so lucky to have a man like him, who would let me be me, rather than try to tame me…

Mr. Murdoch stepped up out of the background, turned off the camera and placed it on the table next to me.

"I think I speak for all of us when I say, we have a deal."

I smiled at him, pleased that they were satisfied, just like I was.

"Thank you. I'm looking forward to our next meeting," I said.

My raise was processed by HR the following week, allowing Gary and I to apply for that mortgage and buy our dream house. Not bad for an afternoon's work…

~ THE END ~

ABOUT THE AUTHOR

Dear Reader,

Thanks for reading one of my filthy tales! My name is Lolita Minx and chances are, as you're reading this, I'm up to absolutely no good. My man, Gary, and I have a special arrangement: we experiment, with ourselves, each other, and a whole bunch of other people whether known to us or complete strangers. Anything goes, there are no rules, except one: we have to have fun. For me, there's an extra layer of fun after the all the decadence and depravity has taken place. I like to write down our experiences, and share them with the world. Check back soon for more dirty tales as I finish writing them ;-)

My stories are available at all major ebook retailers, and I'm planning to release them as audiobooks as well. You can visit my website, below, for more details.

To find out more, check:

eXplicitTales.com

(And why not sign up for the newsletter to be the first to find out about new releases.)

x Candi